THE ADVENTURES OF BUBBY AND DIDI

by
Melissa Gilstrap

Archway Publishing books may be ordered through booksellers or by contacting:

Archway Publishing
1663 Liberty Drive
Bloomington, IN 47403
www.archwaypublishing.com
844-669-3957

ISBN: 978-1-4808-9489-1 (sc)
ISBN: 978-1-4808-9490-7 (hc)
ISBN: 978-1-4808-9491-4 (e)

Print information available on the last page.

Archway Publishing rev. date: 10/19/2020

We are best friends. And we are brother and sister.

We like to go on adventures together. Our "Adventure Box" has everything we need to be anything and go anywhere we can imagine. Our dog, Charlie, likes to come on our adventures, too.

We are going to have lots of fun today.

When we get up in the morning, we are super heroes saving the day.
Charlie makes a great bad guy, because he is super fast.

After breakfast, we are chefs whipping up tasty treats. Charlie loves to try our creations.

While our cookies are baking, we are deputies searching for a bank robber. Charlie is easier to catch when he is napping.

Next, we are a King and Queen saving our castle from a hairy, scary beast. We just pretend Charlie is scary, but he is definitely hairy.

After lunch, we play "Family," which is Didi's favorite adventure.

Then we play "Jungle Hunt," which is Bubby's favorite adventure.

Before dinner, we go on an adventure to space! We love being astronauts, and Charlie does not mind being an alien.

Wherever our adventures take us,
we always have fun together!

We even have fun when we are just being quiet before going to bed.
Books give us ideas for new adventures to go on tomorrow!

Brothers and sisters say goodnight, not goodbye.

I wonder what new adventures
we will go on tomorrow...

Bubby & Didi's Recipe for an "Adventure Box"

Ingredients:

- Large cardboard box
- Old T-shirts
- Cardboard tubes
- Plastic containers
- Dress up masks, clothes and jewelry
- Old Halloween costumes
- Tape
- Box of crayons

Recipe:

1. Gather box and other ingredients. Ask a grown up if you need help finding these items.
2. Put ingredients in the box.
3. Shake the box.
4. Get dressed up.
5. Go on an adventure!

Note to parents:

Unstructured, free play time is an important way for kids to develop many significant skills, such as creativity and how to get along with others. I try to give my real life Bubby and Didi at least an hour a day to go on their own adventures. It is always fun to see what they come up with, and I hope this book inspires adventures for your children as well!

About the Author

Melissa Gilstrap is a genetic counselor at a hospital and mom to her own Bubby (Noah) and Didi (Lydia). She was inspired to write this book because of the adventures she had with her brother growing up and the adventures she watches her own children go on each day. She lives in Colorado with her children, husband, and miniature schnauzer, Charlie.

CPSIA information can be obtained
at www.ICGtesting.com
Printed in the USA
LVHW011232251120
672647LV00005B/307